MUSE

IRIS CARDEN

For all those who dream,

with the hope that your dreams

do not become nightmares.

CONTENTS

Postscript

INTRODUCTION

The boy bounced the ball against the wall. He was bored and wished his mother had time to play. Dad was at work.

Mum, however, no longer seemed to have time for him. She was busy with the tiny, pink object which was his new sister.

When Mum had gone to the hospital to get the baby, she had said it would be a new playmate for him, but the baby was not big enough to play yet. All it did was eat, sleep and cry.

Worse than that, Mum had got a girl baby! He wondered if girl were ever interested in the same games as boys played.

The ball rolled away. He ran after it. Down the driveway and out on to the road, went the ball. The boy stood on the footpath. Mum had told him never to go out on the road. Indecision gripped his young mind, as his favourite toy stayed just out of reach.

"I'll get it for you!" a voice called. A girl, who appeared to come from nowhere, ran out on to the road and retrieved the ball.

"Thank-you," the boy said as the ball was returned to his possession. "Does your mum let you go on the road?"

"I can go wherever I like," the girl replied.

"Gee, you must be old."

"I'm older than you."

"How do you know?"

"How old are you?"

"I'm almost five."

"I'm older than that."

That seemed to exhaust the conversation, but the boy did not want to lose his new companion yet. "Where do you live?"

"Around."

"Do you like to play ball?"

"Sure, I do."

So the two went to the side of the house and together they bounced the ball against the wall.

"Why are your eyes that colour?" the boy asked.

PART ONE

CHAPTER 1

Terry re-read the chapter, selected the whole thing, took one final look and hit "delete". Again. He slammed his fist on to the table. It was going to be another unproductive day, and one he could ill-afford.

The telephone rang. It was Neil, of course.

"How's the book coming, Terry?"

"It isn't."

"What's wrong this time?" Neil had long ceased to sound concerned over Terry's mental block. He was now bored with the excuses.

"I've got the ideas, just no words will go with them."

"I'll send you a dictionary."

"Not funny."

"No, it's long past funny. You know the contract expires at the end of the month and it's the twentieth now."

"I know."

"You've got ten days to get it in."

"I know that."

"I might be able to extend it one or two days for you, but there are people above me, so I can't promise anything."

"What if I don't get it in until later?"

"Don't think of that as an option. The contract runs out. Then anything you submit has to go through the process of being accepted or rejected all over again. Only we've already paid you a fair bit of money – if it's rejected you get to pay it back. I assume paying it back won't be a problem?"

"You know it will be a problem."

"So, get it done."

"Can you try to get me some more time? A couple of extra weeks? Have the contract extended or something?"

"Terry I can try, but I can't offer promises. I'll talk to a couple of people, and since it's you, they'll probably say 'no'. But I'll try, I'll get back to you."

"Thanks."

"Don't thank me yet. I'll call you and let you know how I get on. But work on the basis that the deadline isn't likely to change. Keep writing."

"Yeah, I will, but there doesn't seem to be much point in it."

"Then do it for the fun of it."

"Fun?"

"You told me you enjoyed writing."

"That was when I had a successful book on the market."

"Money makes the difference?"

"When you can't pay the rent, it does."

"Sad story. Pity you didn't, I don't know, save something, when your book was selling so well. I'll let you know what happens with the contract. 'Bye."

"Yeah, 'bye Neil." Terry put down the phone and thought about the money he owed Telstra for it. It would not be long, he decided, until he lost it.

While thinking of things he could lose, he wondered if Nettie would lend him the money for the rent again this month.

He dialled the number. A voice purred, "Good morning, Perfection Modelling Agency, can I help you?"

"Annette Dixon's office, please," Terry responded.

"Who shall I say is calling?"

"Terry Dixon."

The purr turned into a snarl. "One moment please."

Terry tapped the desk with his fingernails. He did not enjoy asking his little sister for hand-outs, but it had to be done.

"Hello Terry," Nettie's bright voice greeted him.

"Hi Nettie, I was wondering..."

"No, I'm afraid I don't have a job for you, unless you lose about five kilos."

"Thanks Nettie, but I don't think I'm the right type. I'm more intellectual than physical."

"No, I'm serious. We need someone for a series of ads for a new brand of office equipment. If you could drop five kilos in the next three weeks, we could use you."

"Well, it's tempting, but I don't think I'm all that photogenic."

"It has to give you a better income than writing – which at the moment is paying you what? Nothing? How much do you want this time?"

"About three hundred."

"Terry, you know, sooner or later, I'm not going to be able to support you."

"I'm sorry, Nettie, but the rent's just gone up. There's nothing I can do about it."

"How about getting a job?"

"I've got a job."

"What you've got is a worthless piece of paper."

"It's a contract!"

"They can still reject the book."

"Only if it isn't up to standard."

"Is it?"

Silence.

"Well, is it?"

"I don't know."

"Look, Terry, I've got to go. There's a client on the other line. I'll call you tonight. Good-bye."

"'Bye Nettie."

CHAPTER 2

"Ten days," Terry mumbled, staring blindly at the screen in front of him. He swallowed another mouthful of coffee. Once more he read the last line. "There is a murderer among us." He thought there definitely was a murderer around. Someone had really killed this story.

Terry began to wonder how he could pay back the advance the publishers had given him. A couple of thousand dollars might not go far, but it was hard to come by. He could not even remember what he had spent it on.

Annette had called back and would pay this time, but suggested that he move into her house, so she would have only one rent to pay. Terry declined the offer, knowing that this sister would not be between boyfriends for long, and he would be in the way. He still hoped to find a way to pay her back. She had aired the opinion that pigs would fly backwards first.

"Ten days," Terry mumbled again, and shook his head.

His coffee cold, he found his way to the sink to empty the cup. Returning, he stopped in front of the mirror.

If the eyes really were the mirror of the soul, then Terrence Dixon's soul definitely needed some sleep.

"You know," Terry informed the mirror, "If my life were a Greek play or a fairy tale, a god or a fairy godmother would show up just about now and all my problems would magically disappear."

For a moment, Terry considered whether talking to mirrors was a sign of insanity. He decided it was merely artistic eccentricity and tiredness. A glance at his desk served to further convince him that what he really needed was some sleep.

As Terry lay down, he felt some remorse that he could not write and sleep at the same time, but all thoughts of writing faded into oblivion as the soothing fingers of sleep massaged his mind.

CHAPTER 3

Terry was falling, weightless, though space. A black whirlpool spun him around and around. Stars spun with him, in the silent blackness, spinning eternally towards an unreachable vortex. As he spun and fell through the whirlpool, a female voice called to him from the blackness.

"Terrence Arnold Dixon."

"Who are you?" Terry responded.

"You are called."

"Called by who? For what?"

He was now standing still in the emptiness. He could see nothing but blackness, but he could sense someone very close.

Again, the voice spoke. "I can help you."

"Help me with what?"

"With what you desire most."

"My fairy godmother, right?"

"If you wish to think of me that way. I prefer to consider myself an old friend."

"Why do you want to help me?"

"Because I need your help in return."

"Help with what?"

"You will be told when the time is right."

"I can't be expected to make a deal on that basis. How do I know what I'll be expected to do?"

"It will be nothing too difficult for you and the rewards will be great."

"How great?"

"Think of everything you have ever wanted. I'll get it for you."

"Do I have time to think about it?"

"There are nine days before your contract expires. Do you have time?"

"I suppose not."

"Are we in agreement?"

"It will be nothing I can't afford to pay?"

"I will even create the situation to make it easy for you to pay."

"How will you do that?"

"You ask too many questions, my old friend. Are we in agreement?"

"Yes."

Lightning flashed and for a second the woman was visible. The second could have been an eternity, as Terry saw her eyes. They were a shade of purple, perhaps lilac was the closest nameable shade.

As Terry stared at those eyes, he felt them reach out and engulf him. Once more Terry was falling, deeper and deeper into a purple ocean, further and further into those eyes. As he fell, he saw it - his book. In a moment he saw it in its entirety and knew he could write it.

He could hear the characters speaking, feel their fear as they looked around them in search of a killer. It was still his story, but it had taken on a life of its own.

Now he had the right words. Now he could tell his story. Now he could do it.

This was the book, not merely a book. It had the classic ingenuity of Agatha Christie, the suspense of Alistair McLean, the mastery of William Shakespeare, and the absurdity of Douglas Adams, and the whole fitted together superbly.

"The greatest novel ever written." The words flowed through Terry's brain.

He typed as he saw and heard and felt. His hands flew across the keyboard. He didn't even question the computer's presence or stop to think when it had appeared. He typed furiously, as if his life depended on it.

CHAPTER 4

When Terry awoke, he found himself, not in the bed he had gone to sleep in, but at his desk. His manuscript, completed, was printed in front of him.

He scanned the pages. Yes, this was indeed it. All it needed was a dedication. Who should he dedicate it to? To Nettie for all her support? In memory of his parents? He looked at the computer screen a moment, and typed: "To Karlee, my muse."

Who was Karlee? Terry searched his mind for some lost memory. As far as he could remember, he had never met anyone with that name, but for some reason it was connected in his mind with the colour purple. He went to change the dedication, but for some reason it seemed right for the book. He printed the page and placed it behind the title page of the manuscript.

Next he rang Neil's office.

A receptionist answered: "Austral Press."

"Mr Evans' office please."

"Who is calling?"

"Terry Dixon."

"You know, Mr Evans has been getting into a lot of trouble, trying to help you."

"Are you his secretary or his mother?"

There was a clicking sound and then Neil's voice. "Hello Terry, I'm sorry, but I can't get you that extra time."

"I don't want it."

"Can you pay back the advance?"

"Nope. But I don't need to do that either, in fact I can do much, much better. I can give you the book. It's written."

"It's what?"

"Written, finished, all done. It has been completed."

"But how? You couldn't write yesterday morning. You had your infamous writers' block."

"I worked all night, took your advice and just kept writing. It paid off."

"You wrote an entire novel in one night?"

"I had a mental block, that didn't affect my typing speed."

"How soon can you bring it in?"

"Well, if I took a taxi right now, do you think you could...."

"Yes, I'll pay the fare for you, but that is it. No more favours."

"I won't need them."

"Right, I'll expect to see you here ten minutes ago."

"I'm already there."

CHAPTER 5

Annette was reading a copy of the manuscript. "It's good," she said, "but why did you dedicate it to Karlee?"

"I haven't the foggiest," Terry replied. "Who is Karlee anyway? It's just a name that popped into my head."

"Don't you remember her?"

"This name is at the back of my mind, as if I should know it. But I have no idea who the person who belongs to the name is."

"Karlee was your imaginary friend when we were kids, the one you blamed for everything you did wrong."

"How did you remember that when I didn't?"

"You always said it was Karlee who put Ted in the incinerator. A seven-year-old doesn't forgive the cremation of her favourite teddy-bear."

"I remember that now. Mum belted the daylights out of me."

"And so she should have."

"Why?" Terry tried to sound hurt. "Karlee did it, not me."

They laughed. Annette fell silent. "It seemed to me," she said quietly, "at the time of the fire, well not at the time of the fire, but later, I was only young then of course, but it seemed that Ted was sort of like a warning about what would happen to Mum and Dad."

"You're not going to blame me for that as well are you?"

"Terry, don't be silly."

"Grandma always said it was my fault, that I must have been smoking in my room and set the house on fire."

"Grandma was a bitter old woman, who had to have someone to take it out on. Let's change the subject. What did Karlee look like?"

"Believe it or not, she had purple eyes," Terry was thoughtful, something hidden in his mind seemed to be trying to get out.

"I guess an imaginary friend can have whatever colour eyes you choose to give her."

"Nettie, for what it's worth now, I really didn't burn your teddy-bear."

"I wonder who did?"

"I don't know, Nettie. I really don't know."

CHAPTER 6

The book sold. His previous book, although successful, had nothing like these sales.

Almost overnight, Terry was famous. He spoke to reporters and autographed books the way famous authors are supposed to do. He was on a high and it seemed nothing could bring him down, until the day he went to the art gallery.

Walking through an exhibition of paintings by Sandra Johnson, an artist whose rise to fame had been almost as rapid as Terry's own, he was confronted with a life-sized painting of a beautiful brunette woman in a long purple dress, which matched her eyes in colour.

The sight pulled from his memory the dream he had the night he wrote the book, the dream in which he had made a deal with this very woman.

Usually a healthy person, Terry suddenly felt weak, as a wave of dizziness swept over him. He looked at the catalogue. The artist had titled her painting: Karlee.

Terry felt cold. He had made a promise to help this Karlee, but he still did not know what she wanted. Did Sandra Johnson know he wondered?

Neil had mentioned the artist once or twice, she was some sort of relation. Terry wondered if he could arrange a meeting through Neil.

Firstly, however, Terry decided he needed a beer, or two.

Sitting on a bar, drinking perhaps more than was healthy, Terry was haunted by the thought of Karlee.

Was the woman he promised to help actually his imaginary friend from childhood? Did the book, his promise and the painting all mean that she really did exist? Did Karlee put Ted in the incinerator? More importantly, did Karlee set fire to his childhood home and kill his parents?

What was she and what did she want from him?

"What the hell does she want from me?" Terry yelled and everyone in the bar turned to stare at him.

Another drinker moved to sit beside him. "Tough divorce case, huh?" The man spoke sympathetically, if with a slurred voice.

"What?" Terry responded.

"I know all about it, said the other drinker. "Women can be such bitches. You give them a house to live in, and kids to look after, let them have a new dress once or twice a year, let them have everything they need and how do they react?

"They catch you with your girlfriend and it's all over. They drag you through the divorce courts and think they have some sort of right to your house; your money. Let them bring up their brats in the riverbed, that's what I say.

"It's the church's fault, you know, never used to be this way when the churches made them promise to obey. Women used to be beaten to death, rather than break a promise to the church, and that's what marriage should be.

"None of this thinking they can get a man's home. That's what I say anyway. What do you think?"

Well, the drunk had asked. Terry turned to face him. "I think I am very glad that my sister is too smart to get involved with a cretin like you." Terry left, wishing he had thought of a better comment. Nettie would certainly have thought of something more scathing.

On the footpath, a better comeback came to him, and he made the mistake of turning and re-entering the bar. "You know," he said loudly, addressing his comment to the man who had been speaking to him, but ensuring the whole bar could hear. "Maybe you needed a dog instead of a wife! Or were you afraid the RSPCA'd have you charged with cruelty?"

At some point in the ensuing scuffle, Terry was arrested for behaving in a disorderly manner in a public place.

"Two more for you," one of the police officers escorting Terry and his adversary said, as they entered the police watch house.

"Just put them in a cell for now, I'll do the paperwork and arrange their bail in a minute," another police officer, who was sitting behind a desk responded.

The two men were placed in a cell together, and the argument began again. The drunk raised his hand to hit Terry.

Mid-strike, the hand was caught from behind, by the police officer from the desk.

The officer turned to Terry, "Dixon, you're free to go." His voice was slow and deliberate, and Terry saw, with a shiver, that his eyes were glowing purple. "There will be no charges laid against you."

"As for you," the officer faced the man he still held in a tight grasp, "you've just added attempted assault to your disorderly conduct charge. Would you like to try pulling away from me, so I can add resisting member of the police force in the execution of his duty?"

The prisoner shook his head.

The police officer released his grip and turned to Terry again. He no longer used his own voice, but the female voice from Terry's dream. "Keep out of trouble Dixon. Not all minds are as easy to control as the Sergeant's, and you are of absolutely no use to me if you end up in prison. Now go home. Neil is about to ring you with an invitation that you are not going to refuse."

CHAPTER 7

The telephone was ringing as Terry opened the door.

Neil did have an invitation which Terry was eager to accept. There was a party planned that night for Neil's niece Sandra Johnson, to celebrate the success of her latest exhibition. Sandra had read Terry's book and had asked Neil to invite him.

Terry turned on the radio for some music while he dressed for the party. The news began. Planning to change the station, Terry stepped, dripping from the shower. The first news item, however, made him stop before he altered the tuning dial's setting.

The local police watch house had burned down that afternoon, killing watchhouse keeper Sergeant Dave Wilson and three prisoners.

Terry turned off the radio, and wondered, not for the first time, if Sandra Johnson knew what Karlee wanted from him.

At the party, Terry found it was not easy to have a chance to speak to the guest of honour. She was never alone. Eventually, Terry decided to butt in on a conversation.

The very elegant Sandra Johnston was speaking with a rather punkish looking being when Terry spoke.

"Excuse me, Miss Johnson, but I have to speak to you," he sounded like a school child approaching a teacher.

The two people went on talking as if he had not existed.

"Miss Johnson, this is important."

She turned to face him. "Don't tell me... You've found the deeper, more meaningful level of my work and you know everything that went through my mind when I put paint to canvas."

"I need to talk to you about Karlee."

She was momentarily stunned. When she recovered, she excused herself from the punk and led Terry to the veranda.

"You're Terrance Dixon? What do you know about Karlee?"

"I know I wrote a book in my sleep and it became a best seller."

"And I did a series of paintings from a dream."

"Did she ask you for anything in return?"

"She said I'd know what it was when the time was right... You too?"

"Me, too."

"What happens now?"

"We wait, I guess. I think whatever it is, she's serious about it, she just killed four people for it this afternoon."

"She what?"

Terry explained his afternoon as best he could....

They stood staring into the moonlight. "What have we got ourselves into?" Sandra said as she moved closer to Terry. He put his arm around her waist. It seemed the natural thing to do.

CHAPTER 8

A display of Eastern art had attracted Sandra's attention. She and Terry went to the same gallery which had housed her first major exhibition, the gallery where Terry had seen her painting of Karlee. Sandra was looking for new ideas — what she found was something different.

Many-armed Hindu gods stood where, only months before, Sandra's explorations of light and shade had hung.

"I wouldn't want to meet her on a dark night," Terry said of a female statue wearing an animal's pelt around her waist and a necklace of human skulls. She was standing with one foot on a headless corpse, and one of her eight hands held a severed head.

He looked closer. "Shit," he said.

Sandra looked, felt a scream moving from her lungs to her throat and swallowed it. It's Karlee," she finally managed to gasp.

The statue had red, rather than purple eyes, and was definitely not in elegant evening attire, but it was Karlee, and it was standing next to the wall on which Sandra's painting of her had hung.

Terry read the statue's entry in the exhibition catalogue. "Kali, Hindu goddess of destruction, worshipped with human sacrifice."

"Let's get out of here," Sandra said quietly.

"Tea," Terry mumbled. "They say tea is good for shock."

"You can have tea," Sandra replied, "but I think I need something much stronger."

CHAPTER 9

Terry had a strange feeling of deja vu as he entered the bar. He lagged behind a little as Sandra made straight for a bar stool. He followed and sat beside her.

"A beer for me," he said to the barman, "and a...."

"Scotch and lemonade," Sandra added.

"Think you can have a drink without tearing the place apart this time?" the barman asked.

"Tearing the place apart?" Sandra asked.

"It's a long story – that day that we met I told you about it. It's just one of a series of exceptionally strange events. You've had a few of your own."

"You hadn't mentioned tearing any pubs apart."

"I didn't really – it was just the drunk I tore apart, or tried to. He was a bigoted creep, but it was still sad that he died that day."

"When are all these weird things going to stop?" Sandra asked with a shiver.

"Weird things?" the barman asked as he brought their drinks. "In my experience, the weird things only happen after you're ready to leave here."

"Not that type of weird thing," Sandra laughed uneasily.

"Oh, you mean this type of weird thing," the barman said as he looked up. His eyes were glowing purple. "As the old saying goes – you ain't seen nothing yet."

"What do you want from us?" Terry asked.

"It's not the right time, yet," the barman responded with Karlee's voice.

"Time?" said Sandra. "What's so important about time?

The barman looked at his watch. When he looked up, his eyes were back to normal. "Time's quarter past two. Enjoy your drinks."

They did not enjoy their drinks. They did not stay to drink them.

CHAPTER 10

Sandra and Terry had been married for a year and Karlee had not made her presence known since the day in the bar. They each hoped that she would not come back to claim her payment. Both maintained success in their fields and they were as happy as any young couple, probably happier than many.

They, at least, were far from having any financial worries. The news that Sandra was pregnant only added to their happiness.

It was, however, a short-lived happiness.

They awoke one night to find Karlee standing at the foot of their bed. There was none of the dream-quality of Terry's previous night-time meeting with her. She stood, as any human being would, a tall statuesque woman, with purple eyes, wearing a long purple evening gown and a large gold wristwatch.

She looked at the watch and then smiled at them. "It's time." She said.

"Time for what?" Terry asked.

"Time for you to pay for everything I've given you."

"How are we supposed to pay?"

"I want the life of your child."

"We are not going to sacrifice our child to you, whatever you can do. You can take it all back if you like." Terry was shaking as he spoke.

"You've got it wrong," Karlee purred. "I don't want you to sacrifice your baby. I don't want her death. I want her life.

"My time is running out, you see. For millennia your people and mine have lived in harmony in this world. You have known we existed, but you chose to pretend that we did not. Deep in your heart you always knew you did not imagine that movement you caught in the very limit of your vision, the object you found in a different place from where you left it, the child with the imaginary friend that sometimes seemed real."

"Lived in harmony?" Sandra found her voice. "You lived on human sacrifice."

"I've only ever taken what I need to survive. In return, I've inspired your artists for centuries. You knew we were here, yet you did not consult us when you made decisions important to us. Now your people are killing us. Your radiation and poisons make our world uninhabitable. We were friends, Terry, I chose you, both of you, to be my artists. I gave you inspiration. I gave you fame and fortune. Now I require you to give me life."

Terry was surprised at how calm his voice sounded when he responded. "And you killed my parents. Maybe you were desperate, and I guess you have my sympathy. You don't have our baby. You never will."

"You actually have no say in the matter," Karlee responded. "I am merely telling you what I am taking so you know your debt has been repaid. You both already agreed to this, and I did not really need your agreement anyway."

Karlee made a sudden leap towards Sandra. As Sandra screamed, Karlee simply vanished.

CHAPTER 11

Sandra had been sleeping uneasily for weeks. Morning sickness, it seemed, and absolutely nothing to do with mornings. She was usually sick throughout the night.

This night she was dreaming.

She was on board an old, square-rigged sailing ship. The sea was rough, and she was aware that it was dangerous, but she was at the helm and she had confidence in her own ability.

The storm raged on under a purple sky and waves washed over the decks, but this did not affect her position at the wheel.

Even in the midst of the turmoil, Sandra had complete control, all she had to do was turn the wheel ... but the wheel would not turn. Sandra wrenched the wheel with all her strength but did nothing except pull her muscles.

As she fought with the wheel, a wave larger than all the rest rose up beside her, hovered over the ship for a moment and fell.

In the deluge, the ship was overturned. It rolled over and over, helpless.

Sandra was aware she was drowning, as she bounced and rolled with the ship, still desperately clutching the wheel. She was drowning and there were sharks here, she knew. The water seemed to be on fire, but how could water burn?

Above the roar of the sea and storm, and the crackle of flame, she yelled for help.

Something grabbed her. At first, she thought it was a shark, but then she realised it was someone helping, dragging her up from the depths. She awoke to find herself in Terry's arms.

"Are you all right?" he asked her gently.

"Yes, just shaken up. I guess Karlee's really frightened me."

"Me too," he said, stroking her hair, "me too."

CHAPTER 12

If parents typically look forward to the birth of a baby, then these parents were similar to most.

Along with the anticipation, however, came fear, fear that Karlee really would return to claim her prize.

The awful truth did not dawn on them until the actual birth. After all the pain, in the midst of her exhaustion, Sandra reached out her arms to take the small bundle the nurse offered her. A tiny baby girl. A baby girl with purple eyes.

"Isn't she beautiful?" the nurse asked. Sandra neither spoke, nor did she actually take the baby she had reached out for. She pulled her arms back, to clasp her sore and empty abdomen tightly.

"I've never seen a baby with eyes that colour before," the nurse continued. "What are you going to call her."

There was an awkward silence, broken at last by Terry: "Her name's Karlee."

"It's an unusual name, but there does seem something unusual, something special, about your baby."

"She's not my baby," Terry said, coldly.

The nurse looked from Terry to Sandra and back again. "Oh," she said. "I'm so sorry. I didn't mean to.... Excuse me, I have to take little Karlee and give her a bath."

Everyone had gone, the nurse, the obstetrician, even the baby. They were alone. Terry kissed his wife's forehead. "So now we know," he said.

"Now we know," Sandra repeated quietly.

They were silent for a moment, and then Sandra began to cry. "Our baby... She killed our baby."

Chapter 13

There was no alternative, or none that they could see. Terry and Sandra took the baby home with them and resigned themselves to pretending that it really belonged to them.

They soon found that, while Karlee was the most beautiful of babies while other people were around, she was something quite different at other times.

Her first teeth cut through when she was two weeks old. To Sandra, they looked more like dog's teeth than a baby's milk teeth.

Baby Karlee would not stay in a cot but would climb over the side of it and crawl about the house at will. She was often under foot in Sandra and Terry's work rooms, particularly Sandra's.

It was one of those days when nothing was going right for Sandra. The painting she was working on just did not seem up to her usual standard. To make matters worse, she dropped a tube of paint on the floor, and the baby bit it. Most babies could not bite through a tube of paint – but this one did – spreading scarlet everywhere.

Sandra went to the kitchen for something to clean up the mess. Karlee crawled behind her. When Sandra returned to the work room, Karlee stayed in the kitchen.

When Sandra took the cloth back to the kitchen, she found Karlee sitting in the middle of the kitchen floor, chewing on a raw steak.

"That is it!" Sandra said. "I have had about as much of this as I can take! You wanted to be a human baby. Well you can behave like one! You can either go back to the cot under your own steam or with a bit of help from me, but you're going back. You are going to be locked in the nursery while you have an afternoon nap. Got that, precious?"

The baby looked up at her and smiled.

"Have it your way, then," Sandra said. She picked Karlee up. The baby laughed, then sank its long, sharp teeth into Sandra's upper arm.

Sandra screamed and let go of the baby. It held tight with its teeth as Sandra felt the flesh of her arm start to tear.

Terry, hearing the scream ran to Sandra's assistance. He took hold of the baby and tried to pull it away, but Karlee would not loosen her hold on Sandra's arm.

Terry grabbed a frypan and struck Karlee with it. Stunned, the baby let go and fell to the floor.

"You bitch!" Terry yelled at the infant on the floor. "If you were a dog, I'd have you put down!"

He helped Sandra from the room and locked the door behind them.

"What do we do now?" Sandra asked.

"Now? Now we take you to a doctor. They won't believe a baby did this. We'll have to say a stray dog attacked you."

"What about the thing in the kitchen?"

"I don't know. We can't just give it away. If we kill it, that's murder. If we try to bring it up like a real child, we mightn't survive it. And how do we let a goddess of destruction, or whatever she is, loose on the world? What damage would that do?"

"A muse," murmured Sandra. "I think she's a muse, not like in Greek mythology, but whatever ancient thing the myth is based on. She inspires artists: you, me, the person who made the that statue of Kali. She's not human. How can it be murder to kill something that's not human?"

"Do you want to try to convince a court that that is not a human baby? And what if our actual child is still in there somewhere?"

32

"Our child? Could she be in there? Could we save her?"

"We'll think about it later. Right now, we're going to the hospital. You're going to need stitches in that arm."

"I'm not sure there's enough arm left to put stitches in. Funny, though, it doesn't really hurt. It's numb."

CHAPTER 14

They lived some distance from town. Although it was not a long drive, the road had a number of curves and had to be driven over carefully.

Sandra was driving. The stitches had been removed, but her arm still felt a little weak.

Terry was in the passenger's seat, with Karlee in the back in a baby capsule.

"Karlee's behaviour is making me nervous," Sandra said quietly.

Terry looked at Karlee. "She's asleep," he said.

"That's my point. Since when does she behave like a normal baby?"

"Well, she has been a bit subdued since the day she bit you."

"A bit subdued? She's been absolutely angelic. It's totally out of character."

"Maybe she's decided to behave herself?"

"You really believe that?"

"No. If she's being good, there's something in it for her. Maybe she thinks if she doesn't behave we will find a way to get rid of her."

"Maybe. Maybe she has something else planned."

"Well, if she has, she's not putting her plan into effect now, she's sleeping happily back there." He glanced back again. The baby capsule was empty. "Where did she get to?" he asked.

"Pardon?" Sandra asked as she turned the wheel. The steering wheel stayed still. Sandra pulled at it, looked down and saw Karlee smiling up at her, as a little hand pulled the steering wheel in the opposite direction.

It was too late to use the brake, too late to do anything. Sandra fought for control, but the car left the road, went over an embankment, rolled over three times, and came to a standstill.

A door opened. The baby crawled out and sat down, chewing a lump of raw meat.

The car exploded in a fireball.

CHAPTER 15

Annette placed the flowers on her brother and sister-in-law's grave.

She still felt she was suffering from shock, after being called in the middle of the night to identify the two badly burned bodies.

The accident had happened some time before the car was found, and animals had already started to eat Sandra's body.

Annette tried to wipe the memory from her mind. Somehow, she could not, not any more than she could wipe out the feeling that Terry was trying to tell her something.

So often, in the three weeks since the funeral, she had felt that he was there with her and that he wanted her to do something.

It was as if he was very anxious or upset about something. There was something she had to do for him.

"Terry," she said to the grave, "I wish I knew what you wanted. I would like to help, really, I would, you know that. I really don't understand what you are trying to say."

A baby started to cry.

"Was it Karlee?" Annette said. "Don't worry about her. She was thrown clear, didn't even get scratched. She's OK Terry, really, she is. Don't worry about her. She's in good hands."

Annette left the graveside and walked over to the pram and looked in. "Don't be upset, Karlee, honey. Aunty Nettie will look after you."

PART TWO

ANNETTE'S DIARY, FRIDAY, JANUARY 20

Dear Diary,

Two more grey hairs this morning! I guess that's what being guardian of a teenage child does to you.

I really thought it was meant to get easier as they got older, silly me! I guess I should be glad that I don't have any of my own to contend with as well.

She said she was going shopping last night with Dave, John and Bill. There were no other girls, just Karlee and the three boys. I tried to explain to her the way people speak about girls who go about with groups of boys, but she told me to stop being such an old cow. How about that?

Anyway, she didn't get in until three o'clock this morning. I asked her where she'd been, and she said shopping. I pointed out that the shops closed at 9.30 and she told me to mind my own business.

I don't know if I've done something wrong. Maybe I should have put her up for adoption instead of taking her on when she was a baby. She might have gone to someone who knew more about kids than I did.

Maybe I am doing something wrong. I keep having dreams about Terry the way I did after the accident. Perhaps he disapproves of the way I'm bringing up his daughter.

I am trying my best. I really am.

School starts again on Monday, maybe that will settle her down a bit.

ANNETTE'S DIARY, SUNDAY, JANUARY 22

Dear Diary,

Karlee didn't go to Church with me today. She flashed those purple eyes at me and said, "Be real, Aunty Nett, nobody goes to Church anymore."

So I went to Church on my own and Karlee went to the beach with Tom and Nick. I know who Tom is, but I haven't even met this Nick.

Karlee tells me he's really nice and drives a yellow car. I'm sure I should be impressed by such riches.

I'm buying a new painting for the office. Well, it isn't all that new, it's one of Sandra's. I'm not sure which one it is even. I just told the dealer that I wanted anything he could get that Sandra had painted. Somehow, I think I could cope with Karlee better if I could see more signs of her parents around the place. Maybe I should bring the painting home – maybe Karlee needs some sense of connection with her parents.

Annette's Diary, Monday, January 23

Karlee didn't go to school today. She said she was feeling sick. I couldn't very well force her to go, she may have been telling the truth. Somehow, I doubt it.

Anyway, I offered to stay home from work, and she made it quite clear that she could manage on her own. I offered to make a doctor's appointment and she said she wasn't that sick.

went to work and left her. I didn't see anything else I could do. When I got home this afternoon, she was drunk.

There's never any alcohol here. I don't drink and I don't have the stuff in the house anymore, all of my friends respect that. So where does a 16 year old kid buy wines and spirits? Just about anywhere she wants to, it appears.

Donna, at work, says her kids and their friends have been known to be allowed into any pub or club they want to go into. No-one really checks ID. The people who run those places don't care – it's not their kids doing it.

ANNETTE'S DIARY, TUESDAY, JANUARY 24

Karlee was sick again today. This time I know she was telling the truth. I also know it was self-inflicted.

I took her to school and waited at the gate until she went inside. I have no idea whether or not she stayed there.

ANNETTE'S DIARY, THURSDAY, JANUARY 26

Dear Diary,

I should be going to Sydney tomorrow, but I'm not really sure that I ought to. Does that make sense? I mean that I should go because a major deal hinges on it, but I'm not sure I ought to because I don't know what Karlee will do while I'm away.

She has already refused to go to Mrs Mac's. She says she's too old for a baby itter. I tend to agree on that. Mrs Mac is a wonderful person and she does not need to be subjected to Karlee.

So which comes first, business, or my niece?

I guess it comes down to a question of how much longer I am going to allow Karlee to rule my life.

Sooner, or later, I'm going to have to go back to living for me.

I remember a time when I my worry on the 26th was the Invasion Day or Australia Day issue; when some staff wanted to put Australian flags in the office, and some wanted Indigenous flags. Those were simple days.

Annette's Diary, Thursday, January 26 (11.30pm)

What a nightmare! I went to bed early, planning on getting some extra sleep, because I did decide to go to Sydney.

I dreamed that I was on the plane and it flew into some turbulence. Then the engines seemed to stop.

I went to the pilot to ask what was wrong, and when the pilot turned to face me it was Karlee.

She laughed and said I shouldn't have left her alone. Then she picked up a parachute and jumped out a door in the cockpit.

I saw the purple parachute opening below me as I woke up.

Am I going crazy? Perhaps I should see a psychiatrist while I'm in Sydney. I am going, whatever happens.

Annette's Diary, Saturday, February 4

Dear Diary,

I'm so sorry! If I'd realised, I was going to stay on for a full week, I would have taken you with me.

It wasn't the business meeting that took all the time. I took the morning flight to Sydney and had the deal completed over lunch. No, it was just being away.

I decided to stay on, because, well, because I felt so free. I really didn't realise how much pressure I had been under, it's like waking up one morning and realising you had been living in a prison all your life.

Oh, and of course, there was Jim. Yes, romance! After all these years alone. Well they say life begins at 40, and I don't reach that age until next month. I'm just starting a bit early.

What can I tell you about Jim? He's about my age, dances very well and likes good restaurants.

He's very tall, sorry I've never been very good at judging height (a big problem in my profession) and works as a clothing designer.

Guess who's arranging models for the release of his next collection? That doesn't sound all that romantic, does it? I can, however, assure you that business is only a minor part of our relationship.

Good-night diary. I'll have pleasant dreams tonight.

ANNETTE'S DIARY, MONDAY, FEBRUARY 6

So much for being on Cloud Nine! You wouldn't believe it! I'm not sure I believe it, and I saw it!

Where do I start? I'm beginning to think Karlee's behaviour is not just run-of-the-mill problems people have with teenaged children. I've certainly never heard of anything like this before.

I thought of calling Donna and asking what she thought, but one of the kids involved was Bill. How do you tell a mother her son was involved in something like that?

Kids experiment with soft drugs and with petty crime, I'd heard about that, but a full-scale orgy in my lounge room? What could I do?

Can you imagine it? I walk in the door, briefcase in hand. It's just another ordinary afternoon.

But there, in the lounge room, is Karlee with at least a dozen boys and not a stitch of clothing between them! I didn't know what to do.

To make matters worse, Karlee wasn't embarrassed. She didn't apologise. Far from it! She said: "Aunty Nett, you want to join in? There's plenty go to around."

I didn't know what to say. I didn't say anything, I walked straight past and went to my own room and locked the door. It was as if I was hiding, or a prisoner, in my own house!

I just couldn't believe such a thing could happen!

There was nothing I could do. Nothing at all. I was frightened, frightened of my niece, frightened of the person she is becoming, frightened of those boys she had with her.

Diary, after my promise to Terry just after he died, I really have tried to be the parent

Karlee needed, but I've failed, I've failed so dismally.

Terry, Sandra, wherever you both are, forgive me, please forgive me. I don't know what happened. I tried, really, I did. I'm so sorry.

ANNETTE'S DIARY, TUESDAY, FEBRUARY 7

Dear Diary,

Jim called. Somehow just talking to him makes me feel better. I didn't tell him about last night. I wanted to, but I really didn't know how to say it. He'll be arriving in town on Sunday, so we can do some work on the Monday – working on that parade for his new line.

I invited him to dinner on Sunday night – here. I'm not sure that was a wise move, but it was easy to tell he was fishing for an invitation, and I didn't want to turn him down.

Let's hope Karlee will behave herself. Lately, it's impossible to know what she will do next, actually I dread to think what she will do next.

Sometimes, I'm glad Terry and Sandra aren't around to see what type of person their daughter is becoming.

Donna said something today about Bill going out until all hours of the night and not telling her where he'd been.

I told her he'd been at my place with Karlee and some other kids last night. I didn't tell her the rest. You can't tell a worried mother that sort of thing.

She asked when he left there, and I said I didn't know. I went to bed before the kids left. I wanted to tell her what had happened, thought maybe she could help me sort out what was going on, but I couldn't. I really couldn't.

Why is this happening to me? I really am trying to do my hardest to do what's best for Karlee. I put my life on hold for so long, didn't go out at all while she was growing up, so she always had me here.

Maybe I should have quit work instead of sending her to the day care centre during the day when she was little. What about Jim? Should I start going out again now? She still does need me, doesn't she?

Karlee's going through a very difficult time right now. I know, all teenagers do, trying to understand themselves and the changes they are going through. Maybe now, more than ever, she needs a stable home, to have me here.

Oh, Diary, I really don't know! Do I go out with Jim? I really feel I need to start to have a life of my own again! But what if Karlee's behaviour is because of something she needs from me, something she's not getting at the moment and something she will not get if she has to take second place in my affections?

Annette's Diary, Wednesday, February 8

Dear Dairy,

I thought of calling Jim and asking him not to come on Sunday night, but I decided I really did need to have a life of my own and that Karlee would have to accept it, she's had me exclusively for 16 years.

Had her parents lived, they might have had other children, so she would not have had them to herself either. Maybe that's where I went wrong. Karlee might have been better off with a proper family instead of just me.

Oh Terry, you name your child after an imaginary friend who always destroyed everything she went near, and then your child seems to do the same!

I've done everything I can, Terry, but I really don't think I did very well. I'm sorry. I wanted to be for her everything that we needed and didn't have after Mum and Dad died. I tried to. I tried so hard.

Annette's Diary, Thursday, February 9

Dear Diary,

It's strange, Karlee's principal rang me at work today. He said he didn't like my attitude. I asked what he was talking about and he went on for ages about a reply he said I wrote to his letters. I asked what letters and what reply, but he just went on about what an inadequate parent I was.

Finally, he said he wanted to see me about Karlee's behaviour. I'm to go there on Monday afternoon. What about Karlee's behaviour? What has she done now?

Monday isn't an ideal day for me, after all I have that work to do with Jim, but I'd better go along, even if only to show I'm not such a pathetic parent.

Sometimes I think I don't really care what Karlee does any more. I've been humiliated, offended and now abused, so I guess there can't be much worse to come.

Is Sunday really still three days away? I wish Jim were here already! I wish I could tell him about my problems with Karlee. I wish I could tell just about anyone, just so I didn't have to face it all myself.

I'm sure she's keeping drugs in the house somewhere, not just alcohol, but other things as well.

Annette's Diary, Friday, February 10

Dear Diary,

What a luxury! A quiet day! I'd forgotten what those were like. Nothing went wrong all day.

In fact, very little happened all day.

I did get a call from the art dealer, who said he was fairly certain of getting hold of one of the paintings from Sandra's first major exhibition.

He wanted to know how much money I was willing to pay. I try to be very guarded with such people. Sure, he wants to know how much money he can sell it to me for, before he spends money to buy it, but I don't like to name a price which might be much more than he would have been willing to accept. With my interest in the matter, of course, I'm still going to pay a lot more than most art collectors for one of Sandra's pieces.

I've got the perfect place chosen for the painting already. It will go on the wall directly opposite my desk, so I can look at it for inspiration whenever I want to.

Perhaps, though, I should get one for home as well, or instead. Maybe it would be good for Karlee to see some of her mother's work.

Sandra's paintings are so hard to come by and they cost so much right now. All I have at the moment is the one she was working on the day she cut her arm, didn't finish it.

ANNETTE'S DIARY, SATURDAY, FEBRUARY 11

Dear Diary,

Jim's plane arrives at 5pm tomorrow! I feel like a teenager on her first date!

What will I cook for dinner? I really have no idea! I'm not even sure of what he likes.

I've scrubbed and tidied until the house looks perfect. Karlee asked if the Prime Minister's family was stopping by.

I said I had a friend coming for dinner tomorrow, and suggested she behave herself a bit better than she has been lately.

She said she was thinking of having another party.

ANNETTE'S DIARY, SUNDAY, FEBRUARY 12

Dear Diary,

Well, it went all right, sort of. Karlee didn't have her "party". In fact, she was very polite, and was even neatly dressed.

She did keep referring to Jim's work as "dressmaking", but I don't think he minded too much.

She also started talking about how she was going to go to University to study economics. It was the first I'd heard that she had any plans to do anything other than cause trouble for me.

Does that seem hard on her? I didn't mean it to be. It's just that – well, anyway, back to tonight.

Karlee was perfectly charming all the time Jim was here. He even complimented me, as he was leaving, for bringing up such a lovely young woman. If only he knew!

Anyway, after he left, Karlee started at me, in that odd way she has.

She said he was a nice man. I agreed. She said she didn't think much of his work. I said it was quite an interesting job, and people should make use of the talents they had. She said she was going to be a politician. I said if that was where her talents were, then that was what she should do. She asked what Jim was like in bed. I told her I wouldn't know. She said if I wasn't going to find out, she would.

I lost my temper and slapped her across the face. I've never hit her, ever. I was horrified, but she just laughed at me. Then she said, very quietly and slowly, "You know, Aunty Nett, you are going to pay for that."

Annette's Diary, Monday, February 13

Dear Diary,

Jim came with me to see Karlee's principal. He said if it was going to be a traumatic experience, he wanted to be there for me. I think we may really be in love.

It wasn't that bad, though. Mr Schneider said he had made a mistake. Apparently, Karlee had been to his office that afternoon and whatever problem he had with her had been sorted out.

He wouldn't say what the problem had been, but did point out that Karlee was a brilliant student. I already knew that. One of the infuriating things about Karlee is that she does everything so easily and has never really learned to work for anything.

ANNETTE'S DIARY, TUESDAY, FEBRUARY 14

Dear Diary

Valentines' Day, and I am in love! Whoever would have expected that? I have a wonderful bouquet of roses from Jim. It came with a lovely card saying how much he loves me. It's so long since anything has been about me.

I paid my cheque over today and my painting arrives tomorrow. It's called Karlee, so it can't have really been from her first exhibition. She and Terry hadn't even met when she did the work for that.

Still, I can sort of imagine Sandra being so excited over the baby as to do a painting her – maybe several paintings of her. Only Sandra would have had the patience to try to have a tiny baby as a model for a painting.

ANNETTE'S DIARY, WEDNESDAY, FEBRUARY 15

Dear Diary,

I don't know what to say, I'm still so stunned. The painting isn't of a baby, and the dealer assures me it's from Sandra's first exhibition.

The Karlee in the painting is a woman in about her mid-twenties, who looks like an older version of the real Karlee. She even has eyes that same strange shade of purple.

How could Sandra have known what her baby daughter would look like, or grow up to look like, two years before the baby was born?

I'm so confused about this. I couldn't hang the painting in my office, I found it too disturbing.

I always thought Karlee had been given her name because her purple eyes reminded Terry of his imaginary playmate who put my teddy-bear in the incinerator.

It looks as though Sandra, also, knew a Karlee, someone who also had purple eyes. How could so many people, real or imagined, have the same name and have purple eyes? Karlee's the only real person I've ever seen with eyes that colour. This is really so strange.

I don't understand it. How could such a coincidence happen?

Well, as the saying goes, there are more things in heaven and on earth than are dreamt of in our philosophy, or something to that effect. (I think I just butchered Shakespeare somewhere there.)

Good-night Diary, I am just so tired.

Annette's Diary, Saturday, February 18

Dear Diary,

Sorry, I've neglected you again.

Karlee didn't come home last night, or rather she came home early this morning after going out last night.

She was such a mess. There was mud over her shoes and legs. She said she had gone out with this Nick person, the one with the yellow car.

Anyway, he drove the yellow car a park along the riverbank, and Karlee says he tried to push her further than she wanted to go. After the events in the lounge room the other night, that really surprised me.

She said she had slapped him across the face and had had to walk all the way home.

I must say, Karlee certainly looked as if she had spent a rough evening. I helped her clean up and gave her a meal before she went to bed.

BODY FOUND IN BRISBANE RIVER.

Police yesterday found the body of a teenage boy floating in the Brisbane River.

Inspector Rodney Alwich, of Brisbane Criminal Investigation Branch said the youth, who had not yet been identified, was aged about 17 years.

He said the body had been in the water for at least 24 hours and showed signs of having been attacked by an animal, possibly a shark, at some stage.

The body was found by a family having a picnic in a riverside park.

Annette's Diary, Monday, February 20

Dear Diary,

You would not believe what was in today's newspaper. Some boy was killed at the river. Maybe even near where Karlee was on Friday night. Attacked by some sort of animal, apparently. They think it was sharks – sharks have been known to come up the river at times. I must speak to Karlee, tell her to be careful of where she goes of a nighttime.

COURIER MAIL, TUESDAY, FEBRUARY 21

TEENAGER IS IDENTIFIED

Police yesterday released the name of the youth found dead in the Brisbane River on Sunday.

He was Nicholas Travers, 19, a first-year university student.

Inspector Rodney Alwich of Brisbane Criminal Investigation Branch said the youth's identity through the registration of a car which was found in the river during a search of the area yesterday.

Because the car appeared deliberately driven into the river, Insp. Alwich said police would treat the matter as a murder investigation.

ANNETTE'S DIARY, TUESDAY, FEBRUARY 21

Dear Diary,

The name of that boy who died at the river was Nicholas. He had a car. Sound familiar? I wonder if it was yellow.

I tried to press Karlee for more information about what actually happened that night, but Jim was here for dinner.

Karlee started to cry, saying a friend had died and awful death and I shouldn't make it worse.

Jim put his arm around her to comfort her and she was crying on his shoulder.

I said if Karlee was there, she should contact the police and tell them everything that happened that night.

Jim told me the girl was obviously too upset to do anything of the sort. Maybe she was, I don't really know.

Her eyes were certainly very red from crying. It's funny actually, the irises of her eyes seemed more red. With most people it's the whites of their eyes that turn red when they cry.

I really would feel more comfortable about this if Karlee would speak to the police. If they at least knew when the boy was last seen alive, it might help their investigation, mightn't it?

The thought of a murder in the middle of the city, makes the whole place seem sinister.

ANNETTE'S DIARY, WEDNESDAY, FEBRUARY 22

Dear Diary,

I had another attempt to speak to Karlee today about going to the police. She said if she did that, they might think she had something to do with Nick's death.

I told her that if she did not talk to them, and they found out she'd been there, they would still think she had something to do with Nick's death.

"You're such an old fool, Aunty Nett," she said. "the police won't know if they're not told."

I had never thought of myself as old until then. Maybe I have aged, more than need be. All the time I could have been having fun, having a normal life, I gave up for Karlee.

I jumped from my early 20s to middle age with no gaps in between, now I'm having trouble trying to find the bit I missed in the middle.

Annette's Diary, Thursday, February 23

Dear Diary

It's very strange! (Isn't everything lately?) I got to work, and that painting was on my office wall, opposite my desk!

I asked everyone and nobody had put it there, or at least nobody admitted to putting it there. Donna commented that it was a good likeness of Karlee, but it it seemed a little older than she should have looked.

I didn't tell her it was one of Sandra's paintings. It is Karlee, and anyone who knows Karlee would have to recognise it. I would feel stupid saying Karlee had not even been conceived, let alone born, when it was painted.

I tried to find out if Donna knew anything about this Nick who was killed. She said Bill had told her that Nick was into drugs, hard drugs, but that was all she knew about him.

I told Donna what Karlee had told me about being with him that night and walking home.

Donna agreed with me that the police should really be told, but she also agreed that if Karlee wasn't willing to speak to them, it was pretty pointless me trying to tell them what she had said.

Sometimes I don't know what is right or wrong any more.

Annette's Diary, Friday, February 24

Dear Diary,

Karlee has been suspended from school for a week. Believe it or not, her grades are still the top for her class, but as Mr Schneider said to me on the telephone, selling marijuana at lunch time was not really approved under school policy.

Unless Karlee learns to behave herself, the next suspension will be permanent.

I remember a time when, no matter what, you simply couldn't suspend a child from school, or did that apply only to state schools? Or maybe that was just a myth.

Anyway, it appears I'm paying thousands of dollars a semester for Karlee to go to an exclusive school and sell drugs between classes!

I asked her why she had done it and she said she was doing an in-depth study in economics. She said she had worked out how to solve the country's economic problems.

I said that couldn't include illegal drugs.

It could, she said, if the drugs were legalised and taxed.

I told her she was lucky the principal simply suspended her and didn't call the police.

She asked why I was so preoccupied with police lately.

I told her she was grounded for a week, and she told me she was going to Mr Schneider's home to apologise if that would make me feel better.

Yes, I said, I guess that would make me feel better.

I am beginning to feel sorry for Mr Schneider and all of his teaching staff. It must be horrible, having to put up with Karlee all day, even if she does have top marks in every subject.

Courier Mail, Saturday, February 25

SECOND RIVER DEATH IN THE SAME WEEK

A second body has been found in the Brisbane River.

The body of school principal Owen Edward Schneider, 54, was found floating face down in the river late yesterday afternoon.

Inspector Rodney Alwich of Brisbane Criminal Investigation Branch said the body had been found by a person who was fishing in the area, at about 6pm yesterday.

As with the body of Nicholas Travers, found in the river on Sunday, Schneider's body appeared to have been partly eaten by an animal of some sort.

While investigations into the deaths were continuing, Insp. Alwich said he did not believe there was a danger to the general public.

He did, however, request the public stay away from the riverbank area near Gardens Point during investigations, so as to avoid disturbing any evidence.

Insp. Alwich said not only were police looking for a human element in the deaths, but they were also trying to find out what type of animal had attacked the bodies.

He said the wounds on Travers' body had been found to be inconsistent with crocodile bites, and neither crocodiles nor sharks had ever been known in that part of the river.

"That's another reason to stay away from this area," he said. "There is something here; something very savage and with sharp teeth. As yet we don't know what it is, and we don't want anyone to be hurt trying to find out.

"Expert marine biologists are trying to identify the animal from its bite marks, and fisheries officers are searching for it.

"That will leave CIB and uniformed officers to search for a human element in these deaths."

He said police still believed there was a human element in the deaths, because Travers' car had been deliberately put in the water.

Annette's Diary, Saturday, February 25

Dear Diary,

Karlee went to see Mr Schneider at about four o'clock yesterday afternoon. His body was found at six.

Nick Travers went out with Karlee on Saturday night and was found dead on Sunday.

Coincidence?????????????

I don't dare ask her to contact the police this time. I'm afraid I know why she won't do it.

Annette's Diary, Sunday, February 26

Dear Diary,

I have just looked over yesterday's entry again. What a stupid idea! As if a teenage girl could have anything to do with the deaths of two healthy males. Of course, she wouldn't be strong enough to overpower either of them!

Maybe I'm getting paranoid in my old age. I certainly feel old lately. Three grey hairs this morning!

Such strange things have been going through my mind lately, you might think it was me going through the trauma of adolescence, not Karlee. Maybe it is the parents who go through the real trauma anyway.

Annette's Diary, Monday, February 27

Dear Diary,

Karlee, under suspension from school still, said she accepted being grounded and would stay home today. When I got home from work, she wasn't here.

I have no idea where she is. I called the police and said she was missing. They told me teenage kids often chose to be missing and to wait and see if she came home of her own accord.

Annette's Diary, Tuesday, February 28

Dear Diary,

Still no sign of Karlee. Jim suggested we hire a private detective if the police weren't interested in finding her.

I didn't tell him I thought the police might have good reason to be interested in finding her. I wonder if they do.

Surely a missing teenager should cause them some concern after two mysterious deaths in the city.

Courier Mail, Wednesday, March 1

RIVERS OF BLOOD: TWO MORE BODIES FOUND

Police investigating the Brisbane River murders yesterday made an unwanted discovery.

Two more bodies, both beyond recognition, were found in shallow water near the riverbank.

Inspector Rodney Alwich of Brisbane Criminal Investigation Branch, said the bodies were badly damaged from being eaten by an animal, and dental records would be required to identify them.

He said the bodies were of one male and one female youths, each aged about 15 to 18.

The matter was being treated exceptionally seriously, he said, with additional police officers being flown to Brisbane from other parts of the state today to help with the investigation.

He once more asked that people avoid going to the Gardens Point area of the river area to see the site for themselves.

Prior to the recent incident, Brisbane had one of the lowest rates of violent crime of any Australian city.

Annette's Diary, Wednesday, March 1

Dear Diary,

The front page of today's paper scared me a lot. I went to the Police Station and demanded to know, rather loudly actually, if the teenage girl I reported missing on Monday was one of the people found in the river.

I then went into great detail about what I thought of the idea that I should just wait and see if my niece came home, when there was a murderer loose in town.

The young police officer at the front counter was very embarrassed, but not half as embarrassed as I was this afternoon, when a detective came to visit, and Karlee was already home.

Yes, she did come back of her own accord. She looked a mess, with mud through her hair, and I'm sure it was blood down the front of her dress.

She didn't offer any explanation of where she had been. Her eyes seem to be a far redder shade of purple than they were when I last saw her. Do people's eyes change colour?

Courier Mail, Thursday, March 2

RUMOURS RUN RIFE OVER BITE MARKS

Brisbane Police yesterday tried to quell rumours that bite marks on the victims of the Brisbane River murders were caused by human teeth.

Inspector Rodney Alwich of the Brisbane Criminal Investigation Branch said the rumours were just that, rumours.

"They are not founded in fact," he said.

Asked whether he was denying that the marks were cause by human teeth, he said: "Tests so far have been inconclusive."

He said a forensic scientist and marine biologists were examining the bodies for clues as to what animal had caused the damage.

"While we have grounds to suspect murder, there is no evidence whatsoever to believe that cannibalism was involved in any of these deaths," he said.

Meanwhile, Brisbane City Council has offered a reward for anyone coming forward with information that will lead to a conviction in relation to the murders.

Lord Mayor David Dennison said the $20,000 reward would go to anyone who could give the vital piece of evidence that would lead to a conviction.

He said the Council was very concerned about the incidents and requested Brisbane residents to do everything in their power to assist police in their investigations.

"These tragedies have cast a terrible shadow over our city, and everyone who lives here has been affected," Councillor Dennison said.

"Parents are frightened to let their teenaged children go out unsupervised.

"As a parent myself, I can understand these fears, as can most of the other councillors.

"This series of deaths has also had a negative impact on tourism, with hotels already reporting lower than usual bookings.

"For the safety of our children, and for the sake of our city's economy, we need this person or persons caught as soon as possible. The Council will give the police any support we are able."

ANNETTE'S DIARY, THURSDAY, MARCH 2

Dear Diary,

Karlee is still angry at me for calling the police when I couldn't find her.

She keeps telling me that I will pay for it.

Annette's Diary, Friday, March 3

Dear Diary,

I'm engaged!

How's that for a whirlwind romance! We went for dinner and then went walking, holding hands in the moonlight. That sounds a bit cliché, but it was so romantic.

Jim actually got down on one knee to propose! He had the ring with him, a delicate little cluster of diamonds.

He's decided to move his business to Brisbane. He's already got his assistant organising the move.

I really was walking on air, until Karlee pulled the plug out of my cloud and left me to slither down the drain.

She asked me whether I'd slept with him yet.

I, being honest with her, said I hadn't.

She told me men were only good for two things, sex and manual labour.

How would a teenaged girl know? I foolishly asked.

She laughed in my face, of course. Then she asked me if I was a virgin.

I said I wasn't, but I'd altered my behaviour severely when I took on looking after her.

Karlee laughed so much she almost went into hysterics.

She asked if I went to church because I thought it would be good for her as well.

I admitted that was the reason. After laughing for another five minutes or so, she told me I shouldn't have bothered. She did not need me, and she did not need any good influences, she said, and she slammed the back door behind her as she went out.

Courier Mail, Saturday, March 4

SMALL CHILD IS LATEST RIVER DEATH

A five year old child has been added to the list of victims of the Brisbane River Murderer.

Inspector Rodney Alwich of Brisbane Criminal Investigation Branch said Sarah Anderson, 5, had been found yesterday morning, floating face down in the river.

This was the fifth death in the Brisbane River since late last month.

Inspector Alwich has again warned people to avoid the Gardens Point area of the river, and has requested than anyone knowing anything about the deaths contact police.

Meanwhile the Queensland Government has offered a $50,000 reward for information leading to the conviction of the killer or killers.

This is in addition to the $20,000 reward already being offered by the Brisbane City Council.

Announcing the reward yesterday, Premier Jill Davis said these crimes were abhorrent and the Queensland Government would do all within its power to assist with the investigation.

Annette's Diary, Saturday, March 4

Dear Diary,

Two detectives were here this afternoon. The wanted to know if I had known that Karlee had been out with that Nicholas boy who had been killed.

I told them I had. They wanted to know why I hadn't called them, and I explained that I thought that was up to Karlee to do. That didn't go down very well.

Then they spoke to her for about half an hour. Then they left. They said they would be back.

Karlee told me to be careful what I said to them in future. I'm not really sure what she meant, or what she wanted me to say.

Sometimes I wonder if she was involved in any way with those deaths. She certainly has been acting strangely lately.

ANNETTE'S DIARY, SUNDAY, MARCH 5

Dear Diary,

It's very strange. I know, I've been saying that a lot lately. Jim didn't show up for a date. I rang his place, but he didn't answer. Where could he be?

Karlee seems to have gone missing again, too.

Annette's Diary, Monday, March 6

Dear Diary,

Karlee came sauntering in just as I was leaving for work this morning.

She told me I should have slept with Jim, he was very good

Annette's Diary, Monday, March 6 (11pm)

Dear Diary,

I have spent most of the day trying to call Jim. He doesn't answer his phone.

Karlee laughed at me and said he wasn't answering because he knew it would be me.

What can have happened to him? This just isn't like Jim.

I'm going in to work, I have to do something, or I'll go crazy just waiting to hear from him.

Annette's Diary, Tuesday, March 7

Dear Diary,

What a weird day! Those detectives were back again, to speak to Karlee. They hardly even said hello to me on the way past.

I wonder if they suspect her of having something to do with the murders?

The phone at work kept ringing and when I picked it up it went dead. It happened over and over again! I thought Jim might be trying to call but had a problem with the phone.

Then, just as I was leaving, the phone rang again. I picked it up and a voice that sounded like Terry's, only very feint, said "Don't trust her, Nettie, be careful." The phone suddenly felt so hot I had to drop it. I have a burn on my hand where I held it.

COURIER MAIL, WEDNESDAY, MARCH 8

POLICE FIND ANOTHER BODY IN BRISBANE RIVER, HAVE SUSPECT

Police investigating the Brisbane River deaths have found yet another body.

James Algernon Edwards, 46, fashion designer of Sydney, was found by police early yesterday morning.

Inspector Rodney Alwich of Brisbane Criminal Investigation Branch said the body had been found at about 7am yesterday.

He said police now had a suspect in the murders and expected to make an arrest soon.

TRANSCRIPT, RECORD OF INTERVIEW, MARCH 8

PRESENT WERE: DETECTIVE SENIOR SERGEANT DAVID ADAMS (QUESTIONS), DETECTIVE CONSTABLE FIRST CLASS ROSS SMITH, ANNETTE DIXON.

INTERVIEW COMMENCED AT 0729 Hours.

Q1. Miss Dixon, as I have already told you, I am Detective Adams and this is Detective Smith. We want to speak to you about what has become known as the Brisbane River Murders. This interview will be recorded on an approved video recording device, do you understand?

A1. Yes.

Q2. Throughout this interview, the device will record not only our conversation, but also the clock above your head and the calendar beside it, so that there can be no editing of this tape, do you understand?

A2. Yes.

Q3. What is your full name?

A3. Annette Elizabeth Dixon.

Q4. What is your date of birth?

A4. Twentieth of March

Q5. What is your occupation?

A5. Modelling Agency proprietor.

Q6. At this point, I must warn you that anything you say can be used in a court of law. You are not obliged to continue with this interview, and you may have a solicitor with you if you wish. Do you wish to continue with this interview?

A6. Yes.

Q7. Do you want a solicitor or other person here?

A7. No.

Q8. Where did you spend the evening of Friday, February 17?

A8. At home.

Q9. Was anyone there with you?

A9. No.

Q10. Was your niece Karlee there?

A10. No, she was out.

Q11. Where was she?

A11. I don't know.

Q12. Who was she with?

A12. Some boy called Nick.

Q13. Nick Travers?

A13. She never told me his last name.

Q14. When did Karlee get home?

A14. The next morning, I think. I'm not sure what time. It was a long time ago.

Q15. Do you often allow Karlee to stay out all night with people you don't know?

A 15. With Karlee, it's not really a matter of allowing. I really find I have absolutely no control over her.

Q16. Did Karlee complain to your that this Nick she was out with had made sexual advances towards her?

A16. Yes, she did.

Q17. How did you react?

A17. I was surprised.

Q18. Did you leave the house at all after that?

A18. No, I didn't.

Q19. Did you kill Nicholas Travers?

A19. No. I did not.

Q20. Did you drive his car into the river?

A20. No, I did not.

Q21. Did you know an Owen Schneider?

A21. He was the principal of Karlee's school.

Q22. Did you have any disagreement with Mr Schneider?

A22. No disagreements, no. We did speak about problems he was having with Karlee at school. We spoke twice about that.

Q23. The second time was the day he died, was it not?

A23. Yes, it was.

Q24. That was February the twenty-fourth?

A 24. It was a Friday, I'm not sure about the date. I remember reading about the death in the Saturday's paper. I had spoken with Mr Schneider earlier in the day and he told me Karlee had been selling drugs between classes. That afternoon, I spoke with Karlee and sent her to apologise to Mr Schneider. The next day, I read in the paper that he was found in the river.

Q25. Did you kill Owen Edward Schneider?

A25. No, I did not.

Q26. Did you place his body in the river?

A26. No. I did not.

Q27. Did you make a complaint to police on February twenty-seventh that Karlee was missing?

A27. Yes, I did.

Q28. When did she return?

A28. Two days later.

Q29. Were you aware that two teenagers were killed while your niece went missing?

A29. Yes, I read about it in the newspaper.

Q30. How did you react?

A30. I panicked. I thought one of them might be Karlee. I came up here, wanting to know if she was one of the kids who'd died. I guess I lost my temper a bit. I was just so worried.

Q31. Do you know the identity of the two teenagers who were killed, or the identity of either of the teenagers?

A31. No, I don't.

Q32. Did you kill either or both of them?

A32. No. What reason would I have for killing them?

Q33. The questions are my job. Please stick to giving the answers.

A33. Sorry.

Q34. There's no need to apologise. I realise this is difficult for you. Would you like another drink of water?

A34. Yes, thanks.

Q35. Did you kill a small child, Sarah Maree Anderson, on March third?

A35. No, I did not.

Q36. Did you know the child Sarah Anderson?

A36. No, I did not.

Q37. Did you know James Algernon Edwards?

A37. Jim's my fiancé. Why did you say "did"?

Q38. Were you aware that James Algernon Edwards was dead?

A38. Jim, no. No. He can't be. He can't be, can't be dead. You're lying. You're lying!

Q39. I'm afraid I'm telling the truth, Miss Dixon. Would you like to have a break for a while?

A39. Yes.

INTERVIEW SUSPENDED AT 0846 HOURS.

INTERVIEW RESUMED AT 0925 HOURS.

Q40. Are you sure you're all right to continue?

A40. Yes.

Q41. Would you like anyone here with you, a relative or clergyman perhaps? Or would you like a solicitor now?

A41. No, I'll be fine.

Q42. When did you find out about Jim Edwards' death?

A42. When you told me.

Q43. Did you read this morning's newspaper?

A43. No, I usually read the paper at lunch time.

Q44. Had your niece informed you she was having an affair with Jim Edwards?

A44. Yes, but I didn't believe her.

Q45. Why didn't you believe her?

A45. Karlee says a lot of strange things. She just does it to annoy me.

Q46. Have you had much trouble bringing up your niece?

A46. A bit.

Q47. Have you had difficulties in keeping her away from bad influences?

A47. Sometimes I think Karlee is the bad influence. Now I know what Terry meant when he rang me yesterday.

Q48. Who is Terry?

A48. Terry? My brother, Karlee's father.

Q49. I understood he had been dead for a number of years.

A49. He has been.

Q50. And he telephoned you yesterday?

A50. Yes. That sounds weird. I don't know. It was someone who sounded like Terry. He said not to trust Karlee and to be careful, something like that.

Q51. Has Terry spoken to you often since his death?

A51. No, only yesterday, and straight after the accident. He and Sandra, his wife, died in a car accident. Straight after the accident, I had a feeling he was there, trying to tell me something.

Q52. Terry hasn't, since his death, ever told you to do anything, has he?

A52. No, of course not. I'm not crazy. It was just a phone call that sounded like Terry. It was probably a practical joke. It just seemed like it was Terry because he called me "Nettie", which is what Terry used to call me. My friends call me "Nett".

Q53. Miss Dixon, have you ever had any black-outs, amnesia, any feeling that you have "lost time" somewhere?

A53. No.

Q54. Do you take any drugs?

A54. Only coffee.

Q55. Have you taken part in this interview of your own free will?

A55. I have.

INTERVIEW CONCLUDED AT 1007 HOURS.

SUSPECT ARRESTED AND CHARGED WITH SIX COUNTS OF MURDER.

BRISBANE RIVER MURDER TRIAL JURY RETURNS GUILTY VERDICT

JUDGE RECOMMENDS WOMAN NEVER BE RELEASED

After deliberating overnight, the jury in the trial of Annette Elizabeth Dixon has found her guilty of six counts of murder.

Dixon, 40, modelling agent, pleaded not guilty to all charges at the start of the 10-day trial.

In sentencing Dixon, Mr Justice McGregor said he had never encountered such brutal crimes as those committed by Dixon.

He sentenced her to life imprisonment on each of the six charges, and said her file would be endorsed: "Never to be released."

During the trial, the court heard evidence from forensic scientist Dr Daniel Evans that the bite marks on the victims' bodies were consistent with human teeth.

He said large parts of the bodies had been bitten and torn. Even bones had been scraped by the assailant's teeth in some cases, he said.

The key witness in the trial was Dixon's niece, Karlee Dixon.

Karlee Dixon gave evidence that her aunt had been very distressed at hearing that the first victim, Nicholas Travers, had made sexual advances at Karlee Dixon.

She said Dixon had run out of the house, yelling something about killing him.

Karlee Dixon said there had been a heated argument between Dixon and school principal Owen Edward Schneider, the day he died.

Her aunt had been extremely annoyed at a sexual relationship which had developed between Dixon's fiancé, James Algernon Edwards and herself, Karlee Dixon said.

She said her aunt found out about the relationship shortly before Edwards' death.

According to Karlee Dixon, her aunt believed she received telephone calls from Terry Dixon, Dixon's brother and Karlee Dixon's father, who had been dead for sixteen years.

After telephone conversations with this "ghost" Dixon would become very disturbed and aggressive, Karlee Dixon said.

A recording of a police interview was shown to the court, during which Dixon commented that she had received a telephone call from Terry Dixon.

In the interview she said she had argued with Schneider, had been aware that Travers had made sexual advances toward her niece and had heard that there was a sexual relationship between Edwards and her niece.

She denied all knowledge of both the two unidentified teenagers killed and the five-year-old Sarah Maree Anderson.

Dixon neither gave, nor called evidence, but when called upon to show cause why she should not be sentenced, after the jury had returned the guilty verdicts, she stood in the dock and said she now knew why she had been allowed to live.

She said she had been made a scapegoat, and she would suffer the consequences of another's actions.

Postscript

Courier Mail, Two Years Later

Karlee Dixon, the youngest candidate in this state election, has won the seat of Ashgrove for the New Australia Party.

Speaking at her victory celebration, Ms Dixon said: "I know we've been called 'The Afternoon Nap' by members of some of the major parties. We're a young party. But we're also smart, strong and we have a plan to work to. The people of Queensland have responded to us overwhelmingly in this election. The same will happen in the other states, and nationally. We are the biggest new force in Australian politics – and after this election, the old guys will sit up and take notice."

Ms Dixon is the niece of Brisbane River Murderer Annette Dixon, and is the person who first raised suspicion against her aunt. She is the daughter of author Terry Dixon and artist Sandra Johnston, who both died when she was an infant.

ANNETTE'S DIARY, TEN YEARS LATER

Dear Diary,

I saw Karlee on the news today.

She said she was going into politics, and she did. From State to the Federal sphere, from a minor to a major party, and then into Cabinet, her career's gone without a hitch.

She's back from another of her trips to the latest disaster area. This time it's an earthquake and tsunami in Thailand. The cameras caught her as she got off the plane. Her eyes are red again.

She leaves Australia with purple eyes, goes to some place with hundreds of people dead and dying and comes back with her eyes flaming red again - just as she did after the murders all those years ago.

The media thinks our illustrious Foreign Minister personally rushes to every disaster site because she has some kind of compassion and wants to see aid delivered efficiently. I know the truth. She's feeding. What's an extra death or two among so many?

People think the eye colour thing is just a trick of the light, but I know better. The more human flesh she eats, the redder her eyes get.

I'm here for life because of her first crimes, but she couldn't go on just blatantly killing and framing other people. Sooner or later someone would have noticed that she was somehow involved.

I wish I could warn someone in authority – but who would believe a condemned killer over a Federal Government Minister?

More by this author

Find more books by Iris Carden at www.lulu.com/spotlight/IrisCarden

Supernatural/Horror Titles:

- Hollywood Lied
- Group Meeting

Anthology of short stories and poetry:

- Patchwork

Spiritual (Christian)

- Beside Still Waters

Children's Books:

- Fred Flamingo Wants to Dance
- The Wallaby Detectives and the Tomato Sauce Mystery
- Poetic Pets

www.ingramcontent.com/pod-product-compliance
Lightning Source LLC
Chambersburg PA
CBHW071141250626
47159CB00006B/2256